SOFIA MARTINEZ

Abuela's Birthday

by Jacqueline Jules

illustrated by Kim Smith

PICTURE WINDOW BOOKS
a capstone imprint

Sofia Martinez is published by
Picture Window Books, a Capstone Imprint
1710 Roe Crest Drive
North Mankato, MN 56003
www.capstonepub.com

Library of Congress Cataloging-in-Publication Data
Jules, Jacqueline, 1956- author.
Abuela's birthday / by Jacqueline Jules ; illustrated
by Kim Smith.
pages cm. -- (Sofia Martinez)

Summary: Sofia and her cousins are making a piñata
for their grandmother's birthday party, but when
Bella the cat gets involved, chaos ensues.

ISBN 978-1-4795-5775-2 (library binding)
ISBN 978-1-4795-5779-0 (pbk.)
ISBN 978-1-4795-6207-7 (ebook)

1. Hispanic American children — Juvenile fiction.
2. Birthday parties — Juvenile fiction. 3. Piñatas —
Juvenile fiction. 4. Grandmothers — Juvenile fiction.
5. Cousins — Juvenile fiction. 6. Cats — Juvenile
fiction. [1. Hispanic Americans — Fiction. 2. Birthdays
— Fiction. 3. Parties — Fiction. 4. Piñatas — Fiction.
5. Grandmothers — Fiction. 6. Cousins — Fiction.
7. Cats — Fiction.] I. Smith, Kim, 1986- illustrator.
II. Title.
PZ7.J92947Ab 2015   [E]—dc23
                                     2014025327

Designer: Kay Fraser

Printed in the United States of America.
052017   010525R

TABLE OF CONTENTS

CHAPTER 1

The Piñata

Sofia carried a big bag across the yard to her cousins' house. The bag held everything they needed to make a piñata.

"Do you really think Abuela will like this?" Hector asked. "Isn't she too old for a piñata?"

"No one is too old for a fun

birthday party," Sofia said.

Sofia pulled newspapers,

balloons, and paint from the bag.

Bella the cat came over and tried

to get in the bag.

"Silly gata!" Sofia said. "There is nothing here for you."

"What do we do first, Sofia?" Hector asked.

"That's easy. We tear the paper into strips," Sofia said.

She handed newspaper to Manuel, Alonzo, and Hector.

Together, they made a big pile
of paper strips on the kitchen floor.

"¡Perfecto! Now we need flour
and water to mix for the paste,"
Sofia said.

"Here's the flour," Hector said.
"It's really heavy. ¡Ayúdame!"

Sofia shook her head. She couldn't help him. She was too busy blowing up a balloon for the middle of the piñata.

Hector started to pour the flour into a bowl by himself.

POP! Sofia's balloon broke.

Hector jumped and dropped the entire bag of flour. It landed right on top of Bella.

"Oh, no!" he yelled.

CHAPTER 2

Cat Chaos

Before they could stop her, Bella ran through the big pile of newspaper strips. She was getting flour all over! Little pieces of paper flew everywhere, too. It was a big disaster.

"Grab her!" Sofia yelled.

They reached for Bella over and over. But she slipped through their hands in a cloud of flour dust every time they got close.

"Mamá is going to be really mad," Alonzo said.

They had to get Bella cleaned up before they got in trouble.

"Where are the kitty treats?" Sofia asked.

Hector grabbed a little pink bag from the cabinet. He quickly gave it to Sofia.

"Ven aquí, gata," Sofia said quietly as she waved a treat in the air.

Sofia slowly walked toward the bathroom. The hungry cat followed her right in.

Bella left a trail of white paw prints all over. But that was a problem for later.

"¡Rápido! Close the door," Sofia said to Hector.

Sofia filled the tub with water. Bella jumped into Hector's arms.

"What are we going to do?"
Hector asked. "Cats don't like to
take baths."

Sofia picked up a big brush by
the sink.

"Does she like this?" she asked.

"¡Sí!" Hector said. "Mamá brushes her once a week."

Hector and Sofia sat down on the floor. They took turns gently brushing Bella.

Alonzo and Manuel banged on the bathroom door. "Let us in!"

All the noise woke Tía Carmen from her nap.

"¿Qué pasa?" Tía Carmen yelled from the kitchen.

"Oh, no. We're in big trouble," said Hector.

CHAPTER 3

The Big Mess

Sofia and the boys ran to the kitchen. Flour, newspaper strips, and kitty tracks covered the floor. Tía Carmen did not look happy. And she hadn't even seen the bathroom yet!

"What a disaster!" she said. "What were you kids doing?"

Sofia told Tía Carmen that
they were trying to make a piñata.

"That is a nice idea, but next
time you need to ask first," Tía
Carmen said. "And now you have
to clean up."

Sofia and her cousins cleaned
everything. When they were done,
Sofia asked Tía Carmen for more
newspaper and flour.

"¿Para qué?" Tía Carmen
asked, looking confused.

"A new piñata for Abuela!"
Sofia said.

Tía Carmen laughed. "Silly Sofia. I don't think so. You'll just make another mess."

"No, we won't," Sofia said. "I promise!"

"We really want **Abuela** to have a piñata for her birthday," Alonzo said. "Please?"

"¿**Por favor**?" Hector said.

Tía Carmen sighed.

"Okay. Grab all the stuff you need, and go out on the patio," she said. "I'll keep Bella inside."

This time, Tía Carmen helped make the paste mixture. No flour spilled, and all the paper strips were pasted on the balloon. Not one got in the house.

Sofia's big sisters, Luisa and Elena, came over to help paint the piñata. Everyone worked extra hard to make it special.

"We need to put candy inside," Elena said.

"Everybody gets candy," Sofia said. "Let's do something more unique for Abuela."

"Something she loves," Hector said. "Like playing cards."

It was true. Abuela loved card games. All the grandchildren spent hours at her house playing Go Fish and Old Maid.

"Great idea!" Sofia said. "She will love it! This will be one party she will never forget."

On the day of the party, Tío Miguel hung the piñata on a tree limb. Abuela put on the blindfold and swung the stick first. Then everybody else took turns.

Abuela laughed when Sofia

finally broke the piñata.

"Playing cards! ¡Gracias!"

Abuela said. "I love my party!"

"And we love you," Sofia said.

"¡Feliz cumpleaños, Abuela!"

Spanish Glossary

abuela — grandma

ayúdame — help me

feliz cumpleaños — happy birthday

gata — female cat

gracias — thank you

mamá — mom

para qué — for what

perfecto — perfect

por favor — please

qué pasa — what's wrong

rápido — quick

sí — yes

tía — aunt

tío — uncle

ven aquí — come here

Talk It Out

1. What is your favorite moment in the story? Why?

2. Sofia and her cousins should have asked permission to make the piñata. Why is it important to ask permission and follow the rules?

3. Do you think the mess was the cat's fault or Sofia's fault? Why?

Write It Down

1. Write a paragraph describing your dream birthday party. Who would you invite? What would you have for a theme? What kind of presents would you like?

2. Sofia loves her grandma. Write a paragraph about someone you love.

3. Pick three Spanish words or phrases from the story. Write three sentences using what you learned.

About the Author

Jacqueline Jules is the award-winning author of twenty-five children's books, including *No English* (2012 Forward National Literature Award), *Zapato Power: Freddie Ramos Takes Off* (2010 CYBILS Literary Award, Maryland Blue Crab Young Reader Honor Award, and ALSC Great Early Elementary Reads), and *Freddie Ramos Makes a Splash* (named on 2013 List of Best Children's Books of the Year by Bank Street College Committee).

When not reading, writing, or teaching, Jacqueline enjoys time with her family in Northern Virginia.

About the Illustrator

Kim Smith has worked in magazines, advertising, animation, and children's gaming. She studied illustration at the Alberta College of Art and Design in Calgary, Alberta.

Kim is the illustrator of the upcoming middle-grade mystery series *The Ghost and Max Monroe*, the picture book *Over the River and Through the Woods*, and the cover of the forthcoming middle-grade novel *How to Make a Million*. She resides in Calgary, Alberta.

FUN
doesn't stop here!

- Videos & Contests
- Games & Puzzles
- Friends & Favorites
- Authors & Illustrators

Discover more at
www.capstonekids.com

See you soon!
¡Nos Vemos pronto!